First U.S. edition published 1986 by Barron's Educational Series, Inc.
Barron's Educational Series, Inc. has exclusive publication rights in the English language in
the U.S.A., its territories and possessions, Canada, and the Philippines.

English translation by Sigrid Brügel and Leslie McGuire
© 1986 Verlag Heinrich Ellermann, München
First published in Germany under the title *Es klopft bei Wanja in der Nacht*
© 1985 Verlag Heinrich Ellermann, München

All inquiries should be addressed to:
Barron's Educational Series, Inc.
250 Wireless Boulevard
Hauppauge, New York 11788

International Standard Book No. 0-8120-5732-5 (Hard Cover)
International Standard Book No. 8-8120-1486-3 (Paperback)

Printed in Hong Kong

456   9955   98765432

Who's That Knocking at My Door?

A story in verse by Tilde Michels
with illustrations by Reinhard Michl

BARRON'S

A strange thing happened one dark night,
While snow fell deep, and soft, and white.
Joseph the hunter ate his bread,
And drank his milk, and went to bed.
Inside, the hut was very warm,
But outside raged a dreadful storm.

No sooner did he start to snore,
There came a pounding on the door.
"Who's at my door on such a night?"
Joseph began to shake with fright.

Out the door, who sat there freezing?
A little hare who kept on sneezing.
With chattering teeth and frozen tail,
The hare was frightened by the gale.
He sobbed, "I really hate the snow.
Let me come in, I'm freezing so!"

So Joseph said, "Step in, don't wait!
And though it's really sort of late,
I'll nurse the fire with some wood.
The warmth will surely do you good."

The hare curled up in Joseph's chair
And went to sleep without a care.
Joseph, too, went back to bed
And pulled his blanket round his head.
"Sleep well," he murmured, "and good night."
Soon both were sleeping snug and tight.

But not for long....

Someone was knocking at the gate!
Joseph groaned, "Who's here so late?"
He slowly opened all the locks,
And found outside a sneezing fox.

Fox wailed, "Please let me warm my toes.
They're frozen stiff—and so's my nose!
I'm out of warmth and out of breath—
To stay outside will be my death!"

The hare shrieked, "Don't let *him* in here!
My mother told me, 'Always fear
All foxes! They *love* eating hares!
They're even worse than hunter's snares!' "

The poor fox looked about to cry.
"I promise I won't even try!
Upon my honor I do swear,
I will not eat you, little Hare."
So Joseph said, "Come in—you should!
But don't forget—you must be good!"

The fox lay down by Joseph's chair
And fell asleep without a care.
Then Joseph got back in his bed,
And pulled his blanket round his head.
"Sleep well," he murmured, "and good night."
And all three slept quite snug and tight.

But not for long….

There was a crash! And then a bang!
And then a bong! And then a twang!
A great big thing with lots of hair
Stood in the door—it was a bear!

Poor Joseph gasped, and shook with fright.
Fox thought, "He'll eat me in one bite!"
Hare thought, "He'll eat me, tail and all!"
But Bear said, "It's a *friendly* call.

"I'm frozen. It's an awful night!"
So Joseph said, "Come in—all right."
Then in the corner sat the bear.
(It was not far from Joseph's chair.)

Poor Joseph got back into bed,
And pulled his blanket round his head.
"Sleep well," he murmured, "and good night."
And so all four slept snug and tight.

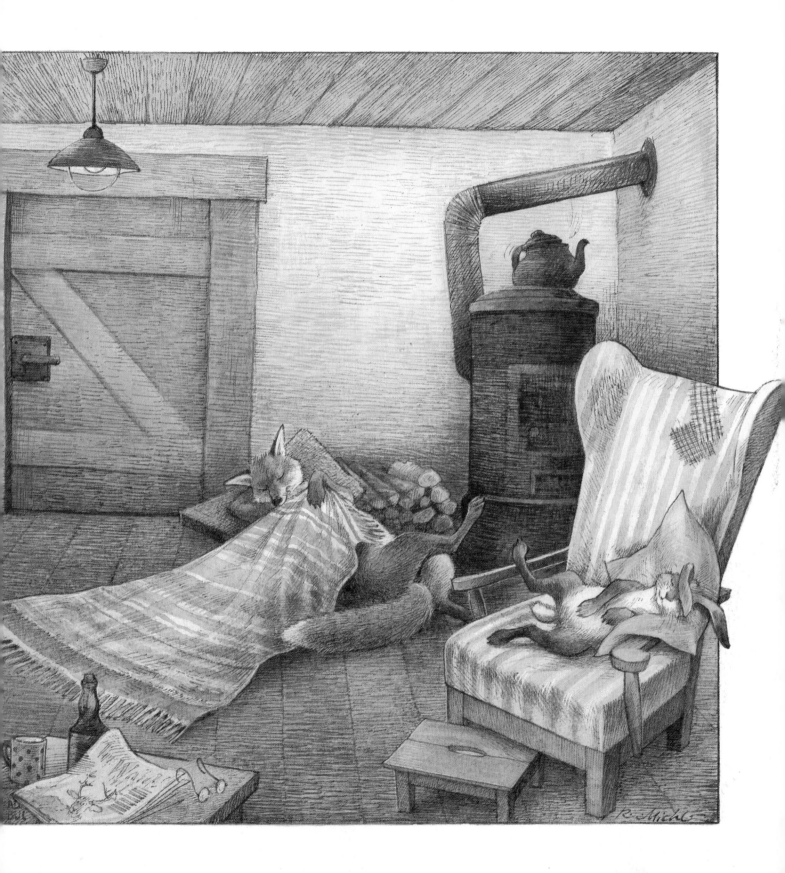

Outside, the blizzard raged still more.
The wind tried hard to break the door.
Inside the hut, Bear, Fox, and Hare,
Slept all night through without a care.

But in the morning, Hare was quaking.
He could not keep his paws from shaking.
" 'Don't trust a fox,' Mom always said.
I think I'd better leave my bed.
I'll find a cozy place outside,
And from this hungry fox I'll hide!"

Fox woke up and rubbed his eyes.
He took one look at that bear's size.
"What awful teeth, and scratchy claws
On every one of his four paws!"

Fox said, "I think I'd best beware
Of this enormous, hairy bear."
And quickly, while the bear still slept,
Into the ice and snow he crept.

The bear kept snoring on and on.
Fox and Hare had long since gone.
Bear's fur and ears felt warm and dry.
Then slowly Bear opened one eye…
And saw right on the wall—A GUN!
"I think it's time for me to run!

"I'm in a hunter's hut, it seems.
I'd better leave, while he still dreams."
On tippy-toes Bear crossed the floor.
He sneaked outside and shut the door.

When Joseph woke and checked the room,
He suddenly was filled with gloom.
There was no sign of little Hare,
Or bushy Fox, or hairy Bear!

"Why have they gone?" he thought. "And where?
Or maybe they were never there.
Was this a dream? I'll look outside."
He saw their footprints far and wide.

"I guess they *were* here after all.
Who would believe a tale so tall?
A fox, a bear, a hare, and me,
Just spent the night in harmony!"

And though the tale is strange, you see
It's also nice—don't you agree?